Red Card

Alan COMBES

Red Card

With illustrations by
Aleksandar Sotirovski

Barrington Stoke

*To Abby, who never flinched from a
tough decision*

First published in 2015 in Great Britain by
Barrington Stoke Ltd
18 Walker Street, Edinburgh, EH3 7LP

www.barringtonstoke.co.uk

Text © 2015 Alan Combes
Illustrations © 2015 Aleksandar Sotirovski

The moral right of Alan Combes and Aleksandar Sotirovski
to be identified as the author and illustrator of this work
has been asserted in accordance with the Copyright,
Designs and Patents Act, 1988

A CIP catalogue record for this book is available
from the British Library upon request

ISBN: 978-1-78112-433-8

Printed in China by Leo

Contents

Chapter 1
Perfect

Seb Brooks is a bully with a big head. I should know because I'm his best friend.

But Seb is fantastic at football. You can't take the ball off him.

He dribbles it like it's stuck to his foot.

He traps it like it belongs to him.

He heads it like it's on a spring.

Seb is the captain of our team. He plays in
the mid-field but he is also our top striker and
he can defend like a pro.

Our coach Jason says that Seb could play for a Premier League team one day.

"Seb, you are the perfect player," Jason told him one time.

"I know," Seb said. "My dad says he's going to tell Spurs how good I am."

Seb's dad says Spurs are the best team in England. That's where he wants Seb to play.

The only place Seb can't play is in goal – and that's where I play.

If a ball gets past me or over my head, Seb calls me "a stupid lump". At first I got upset but then I saw that he gets at everyone in the team.

Here are some of the things Seb said in our game against Red Hill last week –

"Jamie boy, that was pathetic."

"Tommo, we should drop you for the next game."

"My gran could do better than you, Dan."

Seb even tried to bully the coach.

"Jason, I think you should drop Jamie Hobbs," he said. "He was a disaster today."

Sometimes I wonder why I stay friends with Seb. But he's not so bad off the football pitch. You can have a good laugh with him and he pays me back in footy cards if I help him out with his Maths homework.

My dad says, "Someone needs to put that Seb in his place."

But how could anyone do that?

Chapter 2
A Girl

This year has been the best season ever for our team. There are 7 games to go and we're in 2nd place in the league. Our biggest rivals, Granton F.C., are 1st.

"Don't worry," Seb told us all when we were changing for the match against Green Bank Utd. "We'll beat this lot, no problem."

Then Seb fell out with Jason about our game plan.

"You're wrong," he said. "We need to be on the attack."

"Seb's got more cheek than a fat man's bum," Dan whispered to me.

Jason looked cross at Seb. "You're in mid-field," he said. "You can attack whenever you want."

That put Seb in a good mood.

"My dad says I'll destroy Green Bank," Seb boasted. "They're such a bunch of losers."

Green Bank were on the pitch in their green and white stripes when we ran out. The ref was waiting too.

Seb was at the front of our line.

He stopped dead and pointed at the half-way line. When he spoke, the words stuck in his throat.

"No way," he said. "I can't believe it. The ref's a girl."

Chapter 3
Off-side

"My name's Jenny," the ref told Seb. "Do you want heads or tails in the toss up?"

She was about our age, small and pretty with long brown hair.

"Tails never fails," Seb said, like he always did.

The coin landed heads-up in the mud. Seb
pulled a face.

"We'll play with the wind behind us," the
Green Bank captain said.

We had a terrible first half. The wind was blowing about 100 miles an hour. Seb played flat out, but we only got one shot on their goal.

Their first goal was a screamer. I never even saw it.

Then the Bank Street winger got into the penalty area and Dan dived in.

The winger's hand shot into the air. "Penalty, ref," he shouted.

The ref blew her whistle and pointed to the spot.

Seb lost it. "No way was that a penalty!" he yelled.

"It was," the ref said. "Your player had his studs showing."

"Rubbish!" Seb snorted.

"If you don't shut up, I'll give you a yellow," she told him. "I'm the ref, not you."

Seb looked like he might explode, he was so angry.

"Leave it, Seb," Dan told him. "I did it. It was a bad tackle."

They took the penalty. The ball smacked me in the face. It hurt. What hurt more was that it flew into the net.

0–2.

At half-time, our changing room was not a good place to be.

"Cheer up, lads," Jason said. "The wind is behind you now. We'll get the two goals back. No problem."

But Seb was still angry about the penalty. "Girls know nothing about football," he said. "They should never let them be refs. She should get sent off."

No one agreed with him. I thought she'd been one of the best refs we'd had that season.

But Jason was right – the second half was a lot better for us.

Seb was on form and scored after ten minutes. Our striker Glen headed home a corner and we were level.

2–2.

But every shot after that was too high or just past the post.

With one minute left, Liam lobbed the ball to Seb. Seb was un-marked and he took his chance. He volleyed it into the goal and ran back to the middle with his hands above his head.

"No goal," the ref said. "Off-side."

"Never," Seb said. "That was the winning goal and you know it."

"No, it wasn't," she said, cool as ever. "Free kick to Green Bank for off-side."

"Girls don't understand off-side!" Seb shouted. "There's no way that you should be a ref."

That was it. The ref took out a yellow card and asked Seb his name.

"I'm not telling you," he said.

The ref kept her temper under control. "Your name," she said. "Tell me now or it's a red."

Jason shouted over from the line. "Give the ref your name, Seb, and shut up."

Seb did as he was told, but 60 seconds later the ref blew for time.

It was a 2–2 draw and we had lost two points that could have got us closer to the top of the league.

We went back to the dressing room and Jenny the ref went over to one of the assistant referees. I think it was her dad. They both got in his car and drove off.

Chapter 4
Yellow

The next week we played Athletic and I saved a penalty.

This time the ref was an old bloke called Derek Morgan. He was OK, but he found it hard to keep up with play so he often made mistakes. But that didn't matter too much.

We were miles better than Athletic and we hammered them 5–0.

"The ref missed a hand-ball by their full-back," Andy said. "We should have had a penalty."

"And their keeper handled the ball outside his area," Jamie moaned. "That should have been a free kick."

Seb wasn't bothered. He had got a hat-trick that day.

"He was loads better than that stupid girl ref last week," he said. "Let's hope we never get her again."

"How about you think about the next game instead of the referee?" Jason said. "We're top of the league after today. But we have to win next week and we're playing Granton F.C. You need to focus."

Granton F.C., our big rivals. Last year they pipped us at the post and won the league by just one point.

"This season's going to be different," Seb said.

"Maybe," Jason said. "But it won't be easy. They've got Jordan Little and he's the best striker in the league."

"He's not as good as me," Seb said.

"He's got three more goals than you, Seb," Jason snapped.

"That's because he plays up front and I'm in mid-field," Seb shot back.

No one could answer that, not even Jason.

Chapter 5
Trouble

Seb got into trouble at school that week. We had a test on new French words and the teacher found Seb using Google on his phone under the desk.

"There will be no cheats in my class," Miss Martin told him. "You will stay back for one hour after school."

"Get real, Miss," Seb said. "We have footy after school. I'm not missing that."

Seb was in big trouble. His dad had to come into school and Miss Martin told him that she was not being spoken to like that.

"I agree," Seb's dad said, "but can't you punish him some other way? Football is very important to him."

"Good," Miss Martin said. "That means the punishment will hurt him. I'm sorry, but he cheated and then he was rude to me."

Seb's dad went red with anger, but he couldn't argue.

Seb missed practice that night. The next Sunday, Jason had to explain our new tactics to him in the dressing room.

"We can still win this one," Jason said as Granton F.C. ran onto the pitch.

I looked out the window and saw Trouble with a capital T.

The ref was walking out on the pitch.

It was that girl Jenny again.

Chapter 6
Ten Men

Seb used a load of bad words when he saw who the ref was.

"Shut up and focus on the game," Jason told him. "The ref's not important."

"If only," I said to myself.

I could not believe what Seb did before the kick-off. He went over to the ref's dad.

"Have you taken Jenny to Specsavers since our last game?" he asked.

Her dad just shook his head. Then he took out a notebook and wrote in it.

The game was a disaster. Seb tripped Jordan Little after just one minute. Jenny gave him a yellow card. To be fair, it was a bad foul.

Jordan Little soon got revenge for the trip. The ball came over from a corner and Jordan got past Seb and headed the ball into the net. No way could I stop it.

0–1.

"You should have dived, Matt," Seb shouted at me. "That one was your fault."

Just before half-time Seb lost it with the ref. Granton attacked down the wing and passed the ball inside. It came off Tommo, our full-back, and flew past me into the net.

"Off-side!" Seb yelled, as soon as the ball crossed the line.

"It touched one of your players last," the ref said. "The goal stands."

"You are the most useless ref ever," Seb told
her. "Why don't you just pack up now?"

That did it. She gave him a second yellow,
then a red. Then she blew the whistle for
half-time.

Seb got dressed and went home without a word.

We did OK in the second half, for a team that only had ten men.

Jamie scored a great goal and got us back to 2–1. For the last ten minutes we did everything to get another goal, but it wasn't to be.

The end result put Granton F.C. three points above us in the league.

It looked like we would finish 2nd again. We'd need a miracle to be the champs now.

I didn't see Seb for two weeks after that –
he was away on holiday. Then he texted me.

"Granton got beaten 3–0 by Red Hill. Guess
who was ref?"

Jason told us at training.

"That Jenny was ref," he said. "It was a hard game and she sent off two players. Everyone I spoke to said she was brilliant and it was a fair result."

And that result meant we still had a chance in the league.

Chapter 7
Shock

That Sunday, Spurs played Arsenal in the Premier League. I went round to watch it at Seb's house.

"Come on you Spurs," Mr Brooks chanted. He had his blue and white scarf round his neck.

All of a sudden, a row broke out on the pitch. The two captains went for one another. The ref and his assistants grabbed them and pulled them apart.

Seb grabbed hold of my arm.

"Look! Look!" he shouted.

I peered at the screen and got the shock of my life. The ref was a bald bloke with a beard. My heart missed a beat. I had seen that face before.

"It's that bloke," Seb said. "He comes to our games with ..."

"Jenny the ref," I said.

"What are you two on about?" Seb's dad asked.

We told him.

"I bet that's how she learned to ref," Seb's dad said. "Her dad is Guy Rose. He's the top ref by miles in the Premier League."

Seb has been my best pal since we were little kids, but I have never seen him as shocked as he was that day.

Jenny's dad was brilliant. Spurs versus Arsenal is one of the hardest games in the league, but he handled it well. Even Seb's dad said so and he's Spurs mad.

Chapter 8
A Date

We had three matches left in the season. Seb
had to miss two of them because he had got
sent off. We missed him a lot but we still won
both games. 3–2 and 2–1.

I have to say I was brilliant. Some of my
saves were better than the ones you see on

Match of the Day. Even Seb was impressed when he came to watch. Well, he said I wasn't that bad.

So then we had one game left – against Rapton – and Seb was back in the team.

I bet you can guess who was our ref that day. Jenny Rose.

"You need to watch your temper," Jason told Seb. "No sendings-off today. Win this one and we're the champs."

Seb looked along the touch-line. Guy Rose, the Premier League's top ref, was talking things over with Jenny.

From then on it was like Seb was a different player.

If anybody objected to the ref's call, it was Seb who told them, "Shut up and get on with it."

It was a tough game. With two minutes left it was 0–0.

Seb tackled United's striker in our box. Over he went. Seb looked round. Would the ref give a penalty?

No! Instead she took out a yellow card and booked the striker for diving.

I kicked the ball down the field to our striker, Jamie, who was un-marked. He lobbed it over the keeper. With the last kick of the game, we had won 1–0!

We all ran round the pitch like crazy. It was a brilliant feeling.

As we walked off, Seb asked Guy Rose to sign his shirt.

"OK," Guy Rose said. "As you were a good lad today."

"Want to play pool tonight?" I asked Seb, on the way out of the changing room.

"I've got other plans," Seb said. "I'm going to ask the ref out."

"Ha! I've beaten you to it," I said, and winked. "Anyway, she'd have given you another red card if you'd asked her out!"

Our books are tested
for children and young people by
children and young people.

Thanks to everyone who consulted on
a manuscript for their time and effort in
helping us to make our books better
for our readers.

*Also by **Alan Combes** ...*

Josh loves football – but he needs to get much better to play for City.

His granddad has a plan.

Can he help Josh get to play for his heroes?

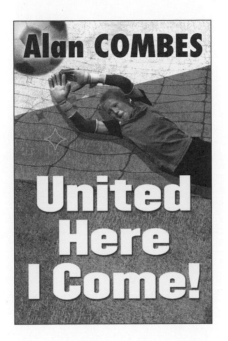

Alan COMBES

United Here I Come!

Jack and Jimmy are very bad at football.

But Jimmy is sure he will play for United one day.

Is Jimmy crazy — or can he make it?

www.barringtonstoke.co.uk